Marty the Maniac

by **Debbie Dadey**

illustrated by **Mel Crawford**

To Marcia Thornton Jones: As E. B. White said,
"It is not often that someone comes along who
is a true friend and a good writer."
Marcia Thornton Jones is both.

Published by Willowisp Press
801 94th Avenue North, St. Petersburg, Florida 33702

Copyright © 1996 by Willowisp Press,
a division of PAGES, Inc.

Printed in the United States of America

2 4 6 8 10 9 7 5 3 1

ISBN 0-87406-772-3

Contents

1
World's Record

"Watch this!" Marty told her friend. Without even touching the handlebars, Marty started to juggle two apples as she rode her bike down the sidewalk.

"Marty, you're a maniac!" Ann yelled. She was riding beside Marty, but she held on to her own bike with both hands.

"No, I'm not," Marty said. "I'm setting a world's record."

The idea of setting a record got started when Marty's brother Frank got a world record book. Frank had bragged about how famous the people in the book were. Now Marty wanted to break a record of her own and become famous too. She was going to juggle and ride a bike longer than anyone else.

"I don't think juggling two apples will win you a world's record," Ann called out, "not even if you're juggling from a bike."

"Sure it will," Marty said. Her bike wobbled, but she kept the apples in the air. "Do you know any other third graders who have done it?"

"No," Ann admitted. Of course, Marty did a lot of things other kids didn't do, like skateboarding backwards and winning the hot-pepper-eating contest at the county fair. Marty wasn't afraid of anything, not even the Lamberts' man-eating German shepherd.

"Then I'll be the first to do it!" Marty glanced at her blond-haired friend and grinned. Just then Marty's bicycle ran over a bump.

Crash! Crack!

The apples, the bicycle, and Marty spilled all over the sidewalk. That's when Marty knew something was wrong. Very wrong!

2
Ouch!

Ann stopped her bike and laughed. "What are you doing now? Trying to beat the world's record for falling off your bike the most?"

Marty stuck her tongue out at Ann and started to get up. "Ouch! My arm!" Her left arm really hurt and Marty squeezed her eyes shut to keep from crying.

"Oh, no! I bet you broke it!" Ann said, looking at Marty's crooked arm. "I'll go get your mom."

"Ouch!" Marty said again, but this time it wasn't because of her arm. It was because she had missed her chance for a world's record.

When Marty's mom took her to the hospital, Marty could only think of one thing: No world's record. When the doctor put a cast on her arm, Marty groaned: No world's record.

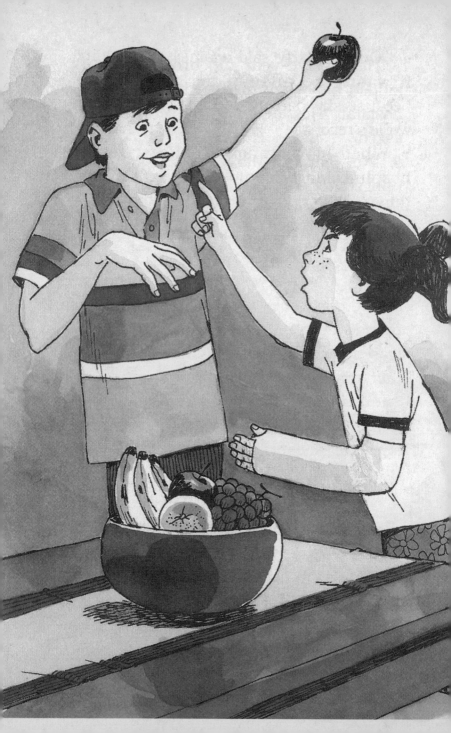

Her twelve-year-old brother, Frank, kidded her when she got home from the hospital. "How about an apple to eat?" he asked.

"No, thanks," Marty muttered. "I'm not hungry."

"I guess the famous Martha Washington won't be able to break a world's record after all," Frank said with a smile.

Marty had never liked her real name, even though she was named after the first president's wife. In first grade, the kids had teased her about it. Marty hated that more than anything. Now Frank was teasing her. She put one hand on her hip and looked him in the eyes. "Oh, I'm still going to break a record," she told him.

14

Her brother shook his head. "You're a maniac. You can't do it with a broken arm."

Marty pointed a finger at Frank. "You just wait. I'm not a quitter. I WILL do it."

Frank rolled his eyes. "Oh, no," he said. "Look out. There's going to be trouble!"

3
The Best Idea Ever!

Marty's cast was white. It was so white it almost hurt her eyes to look at it. But what really hurt was that she hadn't broken a world's record. Marty hated failing. Most of all she hated not finishing something.

Ann tried to cheer her up. They were both sitting on Marty's bed, looking at the white cast. "It's a good thing you broke your left arm," Ann said. "You can still use your other arm to write with. You won't get behind in your homework."

Marty groaned. She hated homework as much as she hated failing. Tomorrow was Monday and she'd have to go to school with a broken arm. A broken arm with a big, white, ugly cast on it.

"Don't worry," Ann told her. "You can break a world's record after your arm gets better."

"But that won't be for six weeks," Marty complained. Six weeks sounded like forever.

"I know!" Ann said. "You could break a record for roller skating the longest."

Marty shook her head sadly. "I'm not the best skater. What if I fell and broke my other arm? Then I'd be in real trouble."

"There's got to be something you can do," Ann said. "Let's think."

The two friends sat without saying a word for several minutes. Finally, Marty smiled. "I could chew bubble gum longer than anyone else."

"Gum isn't allowed in school. You'd get sent to the principal's office right away," Ann said.

"You're right," Marty said glumly. She definitely did not want to go to Mrs. Claret's office. She was the meanest principal ever to stomp through a school. Kids scattered in all directions when she walked down the

hall. And Marty had heard that kids who were sent to her office were never seen again.

Marty groaned once more and plopped flat onto the bed. But she didn't give up. There had to be something she could do.

"Maybe Peter will think of something," Ann said. "He's coming over to sign your cast." Peter lived down the street from Marty and was one of her best friends.

Marty suddenly sat straight up. She looked at Ann like she had just sprouted wings. "Ann!" Marty shouted. "You're terrific!"

"What are you talking about?" Ann asked.

"I'm talking about a world's record!" Marty shouted. "I know what I'm going to do!"

4
Red Marker

"I'll set a record for having the most people sign my cast!" Marty yelled.

Ann smiled. "I guess that would work. Let me sign it first."

Marty got a red marker and Ann wrote her name in big letters and drew two red hearts. **ANN ♥ ♥**

Peter arrived a few minutes later. He came into Marty's room. "Hi, Marty," he said, pushing his glasses higher on his nose. "Sorry about your arm."

"That's okay," Marty told him. "I'm still going to break a world's record. I'm going to have the most people sign my cast."

"I was the first one to sign," Ann told him. "You can be number two."

Peter took the marker from Ann and wrote his name in small letters. "You better have everyone else write little if you want to fit a lot of names on here," he said.

Marty nodded. "You're right. I can't wait until tomorrow. I'll get everyone at school to sign it."

"There are 345 kids at school, not counting the teachers," Peter told her. "I wonder what the record is."

"I'll get Frank's record book and look," Marty said. "But no matter how many people it takes, I'm going to do it!"

Peter handed the red marker back to her. "Just watch out for the principal. You know how strict she is."

Marty gulped. She had forgotten about that. Then she shook her head. Somehow, she'd just stay away from Mrs. Claret. "I'm going to do it," Marty said again. "And this time, nothing—not even the principal—is going to stop me!"

5
A Big Stretch

"Shhh," Marty told Bobby, the boy who sat behind her in class. "Just sign it quickly," she whispered.

Bobby wrote a big **B** on Marty's cast.

"Hey!" Marty said. "Don't write so big!"

"EXCUSE me," Bobby said as he finished the rest of his name in small letters.

"No, excuse me." Mrs. Jones, their teacher, looked up from her book. "We're supposed to be reading, not talking."

Bobby turned red. "Sorry, Mrs. Jones." He buried his head in his book and whispered to Marty. "You'd better not get me in trouble again with that stupid cast of yours."

Marty shrugged and sank down in her seat. She propped her book on her desk and hid behind it. Then she looked at her cast. It had red, blue, and black names written all over it.

Marty grinned. She had 20 names already and school had just started. Too bad she didn't know what the record was. Frank wouldn't let her look at his record book. He hated it when she used his stuff. She'd have to sneak a peek at it when he was outside playing.

Marty peeked over the top of her book. Mrs. Jones was reading again. Marty looked at Nancy, the girl beside her. "Pssst," Marty hissed.

Nancy kept reading.

"PSSSST!" Marty hissed louder.

Nancy looked over at Marty.

"Sign my cast?" Marty asked.

Nancy glanced at Mrs. Jones, then back at Marty. Nancy nodded and took out a green pen. She leaned over to sign Marty's cast. But Nancy was short, so she couldn't reach. Marty stretched her cast out to

Nancy and Nancy leaned a little farther. Nancy still couldn't reach, so she leaned even more and Marty reached farther.

Then it happened. Nancy reached out to put an **N** on Marty's cast. She reached too far and PLOP! Nancy fell onto the floor and Marty fell right on top of her.

Bobby laughed and Mrs. Jones slammed her book shut. Nancy started crying and Mrs. Jones rushed over to help.

"What happened?" Mrs. Jones asked as she pulled Marty off Nancy.

"Marty's cast knocked me on the head," Nancy wailed.

"It's an attack cast," Bobby snickered.

"I was just letting her sign it," Marty told Mrs. Jones.

Mrs. Jones shook her head. "That's all I want to hear about that cast!" she said.

"But . . . ," Marty began.

"No buts," Mrs. Jones said firmly. "Any more trouble caused by that cast and you can take it up with the principal."

Marty gulped. "Yes, Mrs. Jones," she said sadly. Marty looked down at her cast as Mrs. Jones walked away. Twenty names on a cast was not a record. Marty was sure of that. How could she get more names without getting killed by Mrs. Claret?

30

6
Now She's in Trouble!

By recess time Marty had thought of a way to get more names on her cast. She carried a blank poster board and a green marker outside. When Ann came up beside her, she was hard at work making a sign.

"Hey, Marty," Ann said, "what are you doing?"

"Mrs. Jones wouldn't let anyone sign my cast in class so I'm doing it at recess," Marty told her. She held up the sign she'd made. It said, **MAKE HISTORY: SIGN A CAST**.

"Do you think it'll work?" Ann asked.

"Sure," Marty said. She propped the poster against a tree and started shouting. "Make history in a world record book! Sign up now!"

Ann laughed and started shouting just like someone from the circus. "Step right up, folks. That's right, make history here today at Tates Creek School. Be one of the first to sign Marty's cast."

In just a few minutes, kids were lined up halfway across the playground. Ann kept yelling and soon the line was all the way across the playground.

"Let me sign first," a big kid told Marty.

"There's plenty of room," Marty told him. But by the end of recess, a lot of the room was gone. The cast was covered with names from Tates Creek School and kids were still in line to sign.

"We'd better go inside," Marty said when the bell rang to end recess.

"NO!" shouted all the kids in line. "We want to sign your cast!"

So the kids kept signing, even when everyone else went inside. "Marty," Ann said, "we're going to get in trouble."

"Don't worry," Marty told her. "Only three more kids."

"Oh, no!" Ann said, looking like she was going to faint. "We ARE in trouble! Here comes Principal Claret!"

The other three kids scattered like spit in a tornado. Mrs. Claret swooped down on Marty and Ann. Before they knew it Mrs. Claret marched them to her office.

The huge wooden door to the principal's office closed with a thud. Ann grabbed Marty's arm and squeezed. "This is it!" Ann whispered. "We're dead!"

7

How Many?

Marty thought Mrs. Claret looked a hundred feet tall as she towered over the two girls. "Why were you outside after the bell rang?" the principal demanded in a booming voice.

Ann was so scared she couldn't talk, so Marty held up her cast. "We were getting kids to sign my cast," she explained. Her voice squeaked. "I'm trying for a world's record."

"And how many signatures did you get?" Mrs. Claret asked.

Marty turned red. "I don't know," she admitted. "I lost count after 65."

"And how many signatures does it take to beat the world's record?" Mrs. Claret asked.

Marty's face got even redder. "I don't know exactly," she mumbled.

Mrs. Claret tapped her foot, then sat down behind her desk. She folded her hands together and looked at Marty. Finally, she spoke. "I have decided your punishment."

Ann started to shake and Marty gulped.

"No more cast signing at school," Mrs. Claret told them sternly. "And both of you must stay after school today and count the names on your cast. Also, look in the library's world record book to see what the record is for names on a cast."

Marty and Ann nodded slowly. "Yes, Mrs. Claret," Ann said softly.

"Is that all?" Marty asked.

"NO!" Mrs. Claret said. "There's one more thing. Marty, come over here."

Marty walked slowly up to Mrs. Claret, then closed her eyes.

When nothing happened and no one said anything, she opened them. Mrs. Claret was signing her cast!

"I thought she was going to kill us," Ann said to Marty after school. They were in the school library, hunting for a world record book. The librarian was the only other person there.

"I think she will kill us if we get into any more trouble," Marty told her. She found the right book and starting looking through it.

"Maybe this wasn't such a good idea,"

Ann said. "Names on a cast probably wouldn't make it into a world record book, anyway."

Marty held up the book. "Why not? They have one about hiccuping. A man hiccuped for 69 years!"

Ann giggled. "You're making that up!"

"No, I'm not," Marty said. "It's right here. Look, here's a record for the largest cookie ever. It had four million chocolate chips!"

"Mmmm," Ann said. "That sounds like my kind of cookie."

Marty turned another page. "If they can have hiccups and cookies, they can have one about a cast."

"I guess you're right," Ann agreed.

"Here it is!" Marty said a few minutes later. "It's in the kids section." She grinned. "Look. Record for names on an arm cast . . . the record is 437 names in two days!"

"Wow!" Ann said. "That's a lot of names."

"Yes, and to beat the record, I have to finish today, since I started last night."

Ann nodded. "That will be really hard to do, Marty."

"I can do it, though," Marty said. "Maybe I already have enough! Let's count them."

Marty and Ann counted the names five times. Every time they came up with a different number: 361, 275, 169, 189, and 401.

"What are we going to do?" Ann wailed.

Marty shrugged. "I guess we'll have to count again," she said. If she couldn't find out how many names were on the cast, how could she ever break the record?

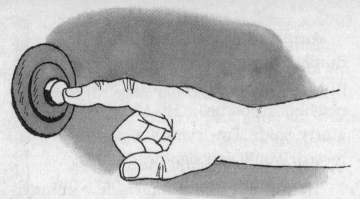

8
Lots of Doorbells

"336. 336. 336. 336," Marty said. "That's it. We counted the same number four times!"

"Finally!" Ann said. She did some math on a piece of paper. "Now all you need is 102 more names to beat the record."

Marty put the record book back and gathered up her school books. "Let's go. I can still get more people to sign before supper."

"But Mrs. Claret said no more signing at school," Ann reminded her.

Marty headed out the library door with Ann beside her. "I know," Marty said. "I'm not going to risk my life for a record. I can get all the names I need on our street."

Ann and Marty ran home and dumped their books on Marty's front porch. Then they rang Marty's neighbor's doorbell. "Hi, Mrs. White," Marty said. "I'm trying for a world's record. Would you sign my cast?"

Mrs. White laughed and her chin shook. "I'd be happy to." Mrs. White signed the cast in fancy writing and drew a flower beside her name. **Mrs. White** ❀

"Thanks a lot," Marty told her. Marty and Ann went down the street, ringing every doorbell. At each house they got new names on the cast. Sometimes they got three or four people to sign at one house.

"This is great!" Marty said. "I should have thought of this before. I'll be done in no time." Marty rang the next doorbell and waited.

No one answered. "Try one more time," Ann suggested.

Marty rang again. The girls were turning to leave when the door opened.

46

A man with tired-looking eyes opened the door. He was in his pajamas, and he was mad. "What are you girls doing? I'm trying to get some sleep!"

"I'm sorry," Marty said quickly. "We were just getting people to sign my cast. Would you like to?"

"No!" the man said loudly. Then he

slammed the door. Marty and Ann walked down the sidewalk without saying a word.

"Marty! Marty!"

"Your mom is calling you," Ann told Marty.

Marty turned around to look. "Marty," shouted her mom from their porch. "Come home and stop bothering people."

"But, Mom!" Marty called back.

Her mom shook her finger. "You come home right now!"

Marty hung her head and looked at her cast. "How many names do we have now?" she asked Ann.

"We got 30 more names," Ann answered. "That means we have 366."

Marty thought hard for a minute. "That means we need 72 more names," she said.

"It might as well be a million," Ann grumbled. "Your mom won't let you ring any more doorbells and we have to get them today or you won't break the record."

Marty did a little dance on the sidewalk. "That's okay," she said. "I'm not giving up. I still have one more idea!"

9

Pennies and Lemonade

"What's your idea?" Ann asked. They were standing in front of Marty's garage.

"A lemonade stand," Marty told her.

Ann shook her head. "What does a lemonade stand have to do with your world's record?" she asked.

"Nothing, except we can use the same idea. We can have a cast-signing stand," Marty said.

Ann looked at Marty. "I think your head is broken instead of your arm. What are you talking about?"

"Just help me and you'll find out." Marty went into the garage and got a big cardboard box and a black marker. She drew a sign on one side of the box. In big letters she wrote, **SIGN A CAST FOR 1¢**.

"You're going to pay people to sign your cast?" Ann asked.

Marty set the box on the sidewalk. "Don't be silly. People are going to pay ME. That way I can keep track of how many names I'm getting. It's easier to count pennies than to count the names on the cast."

"Now I know you've flipped your lid," Ann said. "You are a maniac. No one is going to pay you to sign your cast."

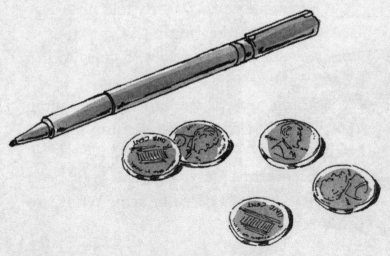

Marty watched two old women as they walked down the sidewalk toward her box. "Hello," Marty said politely. "I'm trying to break a world's record. For only a penny you can sign my cast and be a part of history."

"Is that so?" one of the women said. "I think we can spare a penny, can't we, Virginia?"

The other woman nodded and searched through her purse. In just a few minutes, Marty had two pennies and two more names on her cast.

"Thank you!" Marty said.

A little while later, Peter and three other boys walked down the street. One of the boys bounced a basketball. "You want to play?" Peter asked the girls. "We've got a game up at Nathan's house."

Marty shook her head. "No, thanks. I'm trying to break a world's record today. I need 70 more people to sign my cast."

Peter's three friends signed Marty's cast before leaving. But in just a few minutes, the whole gang from Nathan's house showed up at the booth. They all signed Marty's cast. The pennies were piling up.

"This is great!" Marty said as more people stopped by to sign. One man even stopped his car and got out. "Where's the lemonade?" he asked.

"Sorry," Marty told him. She pointed at the sign. "No lemonade. This is a cast-signing booth only."

The man scratched his head. "I've been all over this country and I've never heard of a cast-signing booth." He chuckled, paid a penny, and signed her cast. As he drove away, Ann gasped.

"What's wrong?" Marty asked. Ann pointed down the sidewalk. Two police officers were headed their way.

10
Oh, No! The Police!

"They're going to arrest us!" Ann shrieked.

Marty swallowed hard. "They can't arrest us. We haven't done anything wrong . . . at least, I don't think we have."

Ann was pale as the police officers stopped in front of the booth. "Well, what have we here?" asked the first officer.

"It's a cast-signing booth," Marty said softly.

"Is that so?" said the second officer.

Marty nodded slowly. "I'm trying for a world's record. For only a penny you can sign my cast."

The officers laughed and reached into their pockets for a penny.

"You mean you'll sign it?" Marty asked.

The officers nodded. "We'll even do better than that," the first officer said. She pulled a radio from her belt and talked into it. "Headquarters, please radio all units near Johnson Street. We have a little girl who needs some help breaking a world's record."

Ann's eyes got big and round as officer after officer showed up to sign Marty's cast. Some came on foot, some in police cars. One even came on a motorcycle. Marty laughed and laughed. Her collection of pennies grew, too.

"Thanks!" Marty yelled as the last police car pulled away.

"That was great!" Ann shouted. "I've never seen so many police in my whole life. Did you get enough names?"

Marty started counting her pennies. She counted them twice and didn't say a word.

"Well," Ann said, "did you make it?"

Marty shook her head. "I can't believe it. I need one more name."

"No!" Ann hollered. "Now what are we going to do?"

Marty sighed. "I don't know. We've got the names of everyone in our families. And we got the names of all of our friends and neighbors, and the kids at school. We even got all those police officers to sign. We asked everyone we can."

"It's hopeless," Ann said. "It'll be dark soon. There's nothing to do but give up and forget the whole thing."

Marty didn't want to give up. She always liked to finish what she started. She stared at her cast for several minutes. Only one name was missing.

"I've got it!" Marty shouted.

"What?" Ann asked.

"I'm STILL going to be famous and set a record!" Marty said with a smile. "I know one more person who can sign my cast."

Ann looked around. There was no one but her and Marty. "What are you talking about?" Ann asked. "Who are you going to get?"

"Me!" Marty laughed. She picked up a red marker and signed her name:

Marty The Maniac

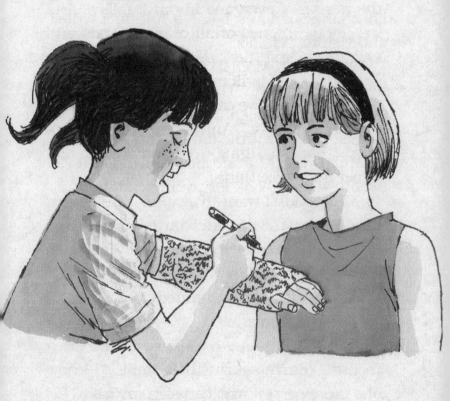

About the Author

Debbie Dadey is a former teacher and librarian. She loves being a full-time writer and visiting schools.

She lives in Morgan Hill, California, with her husband, Eric. They have two children, Nathan and Rebekah. Two dogs, Cleo and Comet, round out the family.

Marty the Maniac is Debbie Dadey's twenty-second book for young readers.